HIDDEN IN THE CHEST

MINECRAFTERS ACADEMY

BOOK FIVE

Winter Morgan

Sky Pony Press
New York

This book is not authorized or sponsored by Microsoft Corp., Mojang AB, Notch Development AB or Scholastic Inc., or any other person or entity owning or controlling rights in the Minecraft name, trademark, or copyrights.

Sky Pony Press books may be purchased in bulk at special discounts for sales promotion, corporate gifts, fund-raising, or educational purposes. Special editions can also be created to specifications. For details, contact the Special Sales Department, Sky Pony Press, 307 West 36th Street, 11th Floor, New York, NY 10018 or info@skyhorsepublishing.com.

Minecraft® is a registered trademark of Notch Development AB.
The Minecraft game is copyright © Mojang AB.

Visit our website at www.skyponypress.com.

10 9 8 7 6 5 4 3 2

Library of Congress Cataloging-in- Publication Data is available on file.

Cover photo by Megan Miller
Cover design by Brian Peterson

Print ISBN: 978-1-5107-1817-3
Ebook ISBN: 978-1-5107-1826-5

Printed in Canada

TABLE OF CONTENTS

Chapter 1: Special Guests 3
Chapter 2: Down the Hole 9
Chapter 3: Treasures and Terror 17
Chapter 4: Rainy Days 23
Chapter 5: Zombie Strike 29
Chapter 6: A Question of Trust 35
Chapter 7: Announcements 41
Chapter 8: Looted 47
Chapter 9: Journey to Mushroom Island 53
Chapter 10: Snowballs and Shelter 57
Chapter 11: Deep Below the Sea 61
Chapter 12: Family Ties 67
Chapter 13: Look Up 71
Chapter 14: The Great Escape 75
Chapter 15: Thunderous Threats 79
Chapter 16: Accidental Answers 83
Chapter 17: Confessions 89
Chapter 18: Farm Life 93

HIDDEN IN THE CHEST

Chapter 1
SPECIAL GUESTS

Julia's heart skipped a beat when she walked underneath the gate that stood at the entrance to Minecrafters Academy. This was her second year at the school, but she still felt a twinge of excitement as she entered the campus. Julia was particularly happy because this year students were allowed to choose their roommates. After sharing a dorm room with Hallie, Julia was thrilled at the opportunity to pick her bunkmate, but there was one problem: she wanted to choose both Emma and Mia, but she could only pick one roommate.

"What are we going to do?" Julia asked her friends as they stood outside the dorm.

Headmistress Lucy stood in the middle of a group of students and called out, "Everyone stand next to the person you'd like to be your roommate."

Julia looked over at Emma and Mia, who stood next to each other. She felt left out, and scanned the area for another friend who might want to room with her. Julia searched through the crowd, but there was nobody. Emma moved closer to Julia and whispered, "We want to be with you. Let's just stick together and see if we can all share a room."

Julia smiled. She knew her friends cared about her, but it was always tricky when three people were involved.

Lucy walked over to Julia, Mia, and Emma. "Would all three of you like to share a room? There's an oversized room that has three beds. I can offer that to you."

Julia unleashed the loudest sigh of relief and looked over at her two friends. Emma had already answered yes.

"Great." Lucy led them to the corner room with four windows.

Mia rushed to the windows to gaze at the panoramic view of the great lawn, dining hall, and other campus buildings. "We have the best views of Minecrafters Academy. Thanks, Lucy."

"All three of you were so helpful to the school last year, and I wanted to make sure you were rewarded."

Emma hesitated. "But we didn't win the Minecrafters Academic Olympics." Tears filled Emma's eyes. "We are a disappointment to the school, and it's all my fault."

"It's not your fault," Lucy comforted Emma. "You were skilled enough to be chosen. The Minecrafters Academic Olympics is a tough competition. We should be proud that our school was even chosen to participate in it."

Emma said, "But I lost the battle. I came in last."

Julia walked over to Emma. "You are a skilled fighter and a teacher."

"A teacher?" Emma asked.

"When I came to Minecrafters Academy, I didn't even know how to use my sword. I'd freeze every time I'd encounter a zombie or a skeleton, but you taught how to fight and to be brave."

"Really?" Emma dried her eyes.

Lucy said, "I must excuse myself. I have to meet my friend Steve. He's going to be a guest teacher here this year."

Mia's eyes lit up. "What will he teach? I want to move past alchemy and try something else."

"Farming. Steve is one of the best farmers in the Overworld," Lucy explained, and then exited the room.

Mia spoke as she decorated her wall with emeralds. "I'm glad there will be a good farming class. I might consider becoming a farmer. Once school is over, I can live on a small farm and sell potions."

Sweat grew on Julia's brow. She hadn't thought about what she'd do after graduation. They had another year left of school, and she was just enjoying being back on campus. She assumed she'd just go back to the cold biome. However, when she came in first place at the Minecrafters Academic Olympics, people from the Olympic Committee asked Julia if she'd build various structures in the Overworld. During the summer break, Julia didn't return to the cold biome, and instead spent the school break constructing a tree house that someone had commissioned her to build. Julia knew she could be a builder when she graduated, and this thought comforted her as she organized her section of the room.

Emma spent a long time in the closet. So long that Julia called out, "Emma, are you okay?"

Emma chuckled. "Yes, I was just inspecting every inch of that closet. After finding Hallie's closet filled with TNT, I was worried there would be something sinister in this one."

"Well," Mia asked, "is there?"

"No." Emma smiled. "It's just a plain old closet that we can fill with our chests."

The group carefully placed their chests on the closet floor as they heard footsteps approaching their room.

"Who's there?" Julia's heart raced. Even though all the excitement from last year was over and the school was rebuilt, Julia was still on edge.

"It's Brad," he answered and stepped inside. "Are you settling in?"

"Yes." Julia was excited to see her old friend. "How are you, Brad?"

"Hungry. It's the First Night Back Dinner. Do you want to go?"

Emma rushed to the window. "Wow, I didn't realize how late it was. It looks as if the dinner has already begun."

They walked toward the dinner as Julia told Brad about her summer and the tree house.

"You know what I had to build this summer?" Brad asked.

"No, what?" Julia replied.

"An igloo. I wanted to contact you for help, but I knew you were working on the tree house."

"You should have asked me to help you. I love building igloos," Julia said.

Emma interrupted. "This is the most lavish dinner I've seen in a while," she said as she pointed at the tables of pork chops, beef, chicken, carrots, potatoes, watermelon, apples, cakes, and cookies. "This is nicer than a holiday meal."

Mia wasn't concerned with the food. She wanted to find Steve to ask him if she could volunteer to work on the school farm. She noticed someone she didn't recognize talking to Lucy, Henry, Max, and Aaron. Mia walked over to them, assuming it must be Steve.

Lucy said, "Mia, this is our new visiting teacher, Steve.'"

Mia introduced herself, explaining that she would love to be considered to volunteer for the farm.

"I thought you were an alchemist," Aaron said.

"I am," Mia replied. "But I'd like to increase my skill set, and farming really interests me."

"I'd love to teach you," Steve said. "It's so nice to see someone who cares about farming. Tomorrow I'm teaching a class on the topic."

"That's on my schedule," Mia said.

"After the class, you can join me on the school farm. I'm looking for other volunteers, too, if you know of any students who might be interested."

Mia didn't have a chance to reply. Two lanky, block-carrying Endermen made their way toward her. One looked at Mia and let out a high-pitched shriek. Mia cried out for help as the Enderman teleported toward her. Her heart was racing. She was trapped.

Chapter 2
DOWN THE HOLE

"Run toward the pond!" Lucy called out to a scared and frozen Mia.

Mia stared at the pond as the Enderman struck her. She was shaking and wasn't sure she could make it.

"You can do it!" Emma yelled, lunging toward the Enderman with her diamond sword.

Mia was still frozen in shock. She looked down at her feet, which seemed to have a life of their own as they sprinted toward the small pond. The Enderman was on her trail, she could feel the purple-eyed creature reach for her. She knew her only chance of survival was jumping into the water. The water splashed her face as the lanky Enderman fell into the water. The water instantly destroyed the block-carrying mob, and Mia was safe. As she stepped out of the pond, Emma and Julia stood waiting on the grass.

"It's getting dark," Emma said, relieved that Mia was okay, "Let's head back before more hostile mobs appear."

Mia stood in front of her, wet and still shaking a little. "Really? You never want to head home at dusk. Last year you used to stay up all night to see what mobs you'd encounter. You usually love battling hostile mobs," Mia reminded her.

"Yeah," Julia said. "Didn't you destroy a chicken jockey on your own?"

"That was last year," Emma replied as they walked back to the dorm.

"Is this because of the Olympics? I feel like ever since that competition, you haven't been yourself," Mia said.

"I just helped you battle an Enderman, didn't I?" Emma was annoyed. She didn't want her friends analyzing why she wasn't fighting.

Mia said, "Yes, but I just sense that you don't enjoy fighting anymore."

"Maybe I'll become a farmer with you," Emma said.

"You can do both, but I want to see you battle again. You're one of the best warriors I know, and it would be a shame to see you stop because of one incident."

"Can we please stop talking about this?" asked Emma.

Students were leaving the First Night Back Dinner as the trio wove their way through the crowd and walked across the great lawn in the direction of their room.

Mia said, "Okay, then we'll talk about farming. I'd love for you to farm with me. In fact, Steve told me he needs volunteers for his farm."

"I'll do it," Emma replied.

"Me too. I'd be up for learning how to farm," Julia said.

"Great. Tomorrow, we will meet Steve after class to work on the farm," Mia said.

The girls crawled into their beds and said goodnight. In the dark room, Julia covered herself in a blue wool blanket and said, "I'm really happy we were able to get a room together."

"Me too," Emma said with a yawn.

* * * *

The next morning, Mia woke up very early to get ready for the farming class. She was excited to start learning about this new skill. Her friends were still sleeping. Apparently, they weren't as eager as Mia. She looked at the clock and realized they had overslept. How could they oversleep on such an important day?

Mia called out to them. "Wake up. We don't want to be late for Steve's farming class."

"Five more minutes," begged a sleepy Emma.

"You need to get up now. You overslept!" announced Mia.

"Overslept? Really?" Emma rubbed her eyes and sat up to see the time on the clock.

"What about breakfast?" Julia asked. "Do we have time to eat? I'm starving."

"I don't think we have time," Emma said, glancing at the clock.

"We're running way too late." Mia handed Julia an apple. "Eat this."

"What about me?" Emma asked as she slowly sat up in the bed.

"This is my last apple." Mia handed it to Emma. "We should pick some at the school farm. Are you guys ready?"

Julia and Emma walked alongside Mia to Steve's class. Emma took a bite out of her apple. She needed energy for her first day at the farming class. Although she wasn't as excited as Mia, she knew that picking up this new skill would mean she wouldn't have to spend all her time focusing on battles. Emma knew that she would miss the thrill of the fight, but Mia was right. After the Olympics she hadn't felt the same excitement about battling hostile mobs. Maybe it was because for the first time in her life, she had lost. Emma wasn't used to losing and she didn't like the way it felt. She convinced herself, that channeling all of her energy into farming would make her feel better. She wasn't sure that it would work, but she hoped it would rebuild her confidence.

"You have to finish that apple before class," Mia said. "I want us to make a good impression."

"Don't worry," Emma said. "We will."

The trio entered the class. Julia knew Hallie was in the bedrock prison on campus, yet she still searched for her face in the classroom. Julia wondered when she'd stop looking for Hallie around campus. It was something she did automatically, without thinking. She hoped by the end of the term, she could break the habit.

Steve entered the class and asked, "Has anyone ever built a farm?"

Shockingly only a few people raised their hands. A boy with orange hair said, "I've spent my entire life on a farm."

"Great." Steve smiled. "You will be very helpful to the class. What's your name?"

"Nick."

Another student with rusty brown hair raised his hand. "Do I really have to be here? Farming is so lame."

"Lame? Do you like eating potatoes and having wheat?" Steve asked the student.

"Yes," he replied.

"You can't have any of those things without a farm." Steve lectured the class on how farms are vital to everyone's survival in the Overworld. He taught them the basics of farming. "Before anything, you must have a seed stock."

As Steve spoke, Mia took meticulous notes. She wanted to learn every aspect of farming, and wanted to be prepared when she finally got to work on the farm. As the class came to a close, Steve announced, "I'm looking for a few volunteers to help on the school farm. If you're interested, please meet me by the school farm following the class."

Mia looked over at her friends and smiled. She enjoyed being in the class, but she was eager to get into the dirt and start planting. Sitting around listening to Steve lecture wasn't as thrilling as she'd expected. Mia thought farming was a subject that was best learned by doing. She also wanted to replenish her supply of apples, and she knew that there were a couple of flourishing apple trees on campus.

Class was over, and Julia walked over to Emma and Mia. “What’s up with the guy who told Steve farming was lame? That was incredibly rude.”

“Yes,” Mia agreed.

The trio entered the school farm, and Julia was shocked to see Nick and the boy from class who dismissed farming standing next to Steve. Steve asked the boy to introduce himself.

“I’m Jamie. We are all going to work together to build the best possible farm for the school. Are you guys ready?”

Mia looked over at Jamie. She doubted he was ready; he didn’t seem to enjoy farming at all. She knew it was a little early to judge Jamie, though. If they were going to work together, they’d need to learn to respect each other. Mia stared off into the distance as Steve began to explain the basics on farming.

Steve held a pickaxe and dug in into a patch of dirt. “We have to start building an irrigation system.”

“Yes, crops can’t grow without water,” Nick said.

“Very good, Nick,” Steve remarked as he dug deeper, but paused.

“What is it? Can we not dig here?” Nick asked.

“No.” Steve stared inside the hole he had dug. “We can, but—“

“Then what is it?” Nick questioned. “Why did you stop?”

Steve leaned over the hole and pulled out a large treasure chest.

“Cool!” Jamie exclaimed.

Steve cleaned the dirt off the top of the chest and opened it. "Diamonds."

Julia looked inside. "And enchanted books."

"I wonder who this belongs to," Mia said.

Julia assumed it belonged to Hallie or some other criminal who was hiding their treasures, but also wondered, "Do you think this could have spawned naturally?"

"Possibly," Steve replied. "Since you were all here when we found it, I think everyone in the group should share the loot from the treasure."

"Wow!" Julia exclaimed. "That's awesome."

As Steve picked up the first diamond from the chest, a powerful thunderous boom shook the campus.

Chapter 3
TREASURES AND TERROR

"What was that?" Julia's voice cracked.

Another piercing thunderous sound shook the ground of the school farm. A lightning bolt flashed across the sky, hitting the great lawn. Rain fell from the sky, creating a flood on the campus. The rain pounded down onto the soggy farm as a skeleton army spawned in the heart of the campus. The skeletons aimed their arrows at the group standing in the farm.

Emma sprinted away from the arrows. Steve called out, "Where are you going? You have to help us battle the skeletons. Every person counts."

"I can't," Emma cried. "I'm sorry, but I can't." She sprinted out of sight, abandoning her friends.

Julia watched Emma sprint away, and didn't notice the barrage of arrows that struck her arm, "Ouch!"

"Put on your armor!" Steve called out to the group.

Mia tried to pull her armor out from her inventory while dodging arrows from the skeleton army. The skeletons marched toward the group, cornering them. Steve looked down at the treasure chest. He wondered if he closed the chest, if it would have any impact on the storm. He realized that it had started when he opened the chest, but even after he reached down and closed it, the storm continued and the skeleton army kept growing.

Julia looked over at Steve. She realized that he thought the chest must have had some impact on the storm. She wondered if it wasn't opening the chest that caused the powerful storm and skeleton invasion, but the removal of the treasure. She called out, "Put the diamond back."

"What?" Steve couldn't hear Julia as another loud deafening thunderous boom roared across the campus.

"Put the diamond back!" she screamed as loud as she could. Another arrow struck her exposed arm. She wanted Steve to place that diamond back in the treasure chest and for this invasion to end.

Julia leapt toward two skeletons, slamming her sword into them. She wished Emma were there to help her battle the bony beasts. Julia knew Emma would have annihilated them in seconds. As four skeletons surrounded Julia, she fumbled with her sword. Two skeletons' arrows ripped through her arms, and her energy was almost depleted. She hoped Steve had heard her and placed the diamond back in the chest. She also hoped returning the diamond to the treasure chest would stop the storm.

Jamie sprinted toward Julia and struck two of the skeletons, weakening them, which allowed Julia to deliver the final blows.

"Thanks!" Julia lunged at another skeleton, destroying it and picking up the bone it dropped.

"Help!" Mia screamed.

Julia looked over at Mia, and was devastated to find her friend in serious trouble. Numerous skeletons surrounded her, and she appeared incredibly weak and unable to continue her battle with the bony mob. As Julia and Jamie raced toward Mia, she spotted Steve picking up the diamond and placing it in the chest.

Julia traded her sword for a bow and arrow and shot arrows at the skeletons that attacked her friend. Jamie and Nick joined Julia and unleashed a barrage of arrows, destroying a few of the skeletons that surrounded Mia. Yet no matter how many skeletons they destroyed, more instantly spawned.

Julia was inches from Mia when the skeletons disappeared and the rain stopped. She looked over at Steve, who called out to her, "The diamond. It's back in the chest."

Julia rushed over to him. "Did the rain stop when you placed it back in the chest?"

Mia stood behind her, sipping a potion to regain her strength. "Do you think we caused the storm when we took the diamond out of the chest?"

"Possibly," Steve said. "But we can't be sure unless I take it out again and we see if the storm starts."

"Please don't," Mia begged.

"We have to do it," Julia said. "Steve's right. It's the only way we can be certain that removing the diamond is responsible for causing the storm."

"Everyone should drink a potion to regain their strength. And keep your armor on and take out a weapon," Steve instructed.

Julia picked a potion of healing from her inventory and took a sip. Steve looked at the group and asked them if they were ready. The gang looked at each other. They shook their heads.

"Okay, I'm going to take out the diamond. Get ready for a possible storm and skeleton attack," Steve said as he pulled the diamond out from the chest.

The familiar menacing sound of thunder shook the campus yet again. Rain pelted down to the ground with such intensity that the pond began to overflow. More skeletons spawned and the gang was in the midst of an instant skeleton invasion.

Steve was about to put the diamond back in the chest, but he fumbled and dropped the precious gem as two arrows pierced through his arm. Julia raced to Steve's side and leaned over to grab the diamond laying on the soggy grass, but as she reached for the glistening gem, three skeletons surrounded her.

"Help!" Julia cried out.

Steve wanted to help, but he was in the middle of his own personal battle, as more skeletons, each one clutching a bow in its bony hand, shot arrows at his exposed arms. Despite drinking a potion to regain his energy, Steve could tell that he was losing hearts. This wasn't an easy battle. In the midst of the battle against the skeletons, he glimpsed a gang of vacant-eyed zombies walking past the Dining Hall. Skeletons weren't the only hostile mobs attacking them! Steve regretted experimenting. He shouldn't have removed the diamond from the chest to see if that was the reason the storm had occurred, but it was too late to think of that now. He had to destroy the skeletons and replace the diamond in order to bring peace back to the campus.

Julia grabbed a potion from her inventory and splashed it on the skeletons attacking her from all sides. She lunged at the weakened skeletons with her diamond sword, destroying them one by one. She wished Emma were there to watch her battle these bony beasts. As Julia rushed back to Steve, she was relieved to see that he had the diamond in his hand. He quickly placed it back in the chest. The storm was over, and the gang let out a collective sigh of relief.

As the campus transformed from chaotic to calm, the headmistress Lucy sprinted across the lawn.

Lucy rushed over to Steve. "What's going on?"

Steve looked down at the chest. "I think we have a serious problem."

Chapter 4
RAINY DAYS

The lunchroom was filled with chatter about the treasure chest. Julia walked through the large dining hall with her tray, catching bits of conversations.

"The volunteers on the school farm were annihilated."

"Really?"

"Someone put them on hardcore mode."

"The campus is cursed."

Julia didn't interrupt the many conversations to tell the students that they were misinformed. Her friends weren't destroyed, and she was standing in the middle of the dining hall holding a tray of chicken and potatoes. Yet Julia felt a lump in her throat when she heard the last comment. It made her wonder if the school was actually cursed. Maybe when Steve opened the treasure chest, he had unleashed a powerfully potent evil force onto the campus? She wasn't sure and hoped this wasn't the case, but she knew whatever the case might be, she'd do anything to help the school. She had been instrumental in stopping Hallie, and Julia was confident she could help again.

"Over here," Emma called out to Julia across the crowded cafeteria.

Mia said, "You can't believe what I heard when I was in line to get food. Two guys were talking about how we and the other folks who were on the farm were zapped out of the Overworld."

"I just heard someone talking about that too," Julia said.

Brad rushed over to their table. "Julia! Wow, I've heard stories about you guys. I was so worried you were destroyed."

"Nope, those were just rumors," Julia confirmed.

"I can see." Brad smiled. "I'm glad you're okay."

"I'm worried, though. I feel that Steve unleashed something sinister when he opened that chest," Julia confessed.

"I agree," Mia said. "That was intense."

Brad looked at his schedule. "Do you guys have Max's modding class on your schedule? I do, and I have to leave now."

"Yes." Julia barely had enough time to eat. She was so shaken by the incident that morning that everything seemed to take much longer than usual. She was still processing the attack when she and her friends walked to class with Brad.

The class started with Max lecturing them on new mod packs and helpful ones to construct for combat. This was when Emma would usually ask a lot of questions about combat, but when Julia looked over at her, Emma was listened silently. In fact, she almost appeared to be sleeping. Julia wanted to call out to Emma and tell her to pay attention.

A girl with black hair and a red hairband walked into the class, smiled, and looked for an empty seat.

Max stopped lecturing. "You must be the new student. Lucy told me you would be arriving today. Please introduce yourself to the class."

The girl stood by her desk. "My name is Cayla. I'm excited to learn about mods and attend Minecrafters Academy."

"We're excited to have you in the class." Max smiled and resumed lecturing the class on mod packs.

After class, Cayla walked alongside Julia, Emma, and Mia as they entered the dorms.

"Do you live here?" Emma asked.

"Yes."

Cayla climbed the stairs, walked down the same hall as Emma, then pointed to the end of the hall. "I live down there. The last room on the left."

A thunderous roar rocked the dorms.

"What was that?" Mia's voice shook as she addressed her friends.

"It sounds like thunder," Cayla said.

The group stood in silence as they waited for another thunderous boom or the sound of rain against the dorm, but nothing happened.

"I guess that was just a random sound," Emma said.

"Yes," Cayla agreed. "Nice meeting you guys. I'm sure I'll see you around campus."

The trio entered their room, and Mia rushed to the window. She saw Steve, Lucy, and Max standing on the farm next to the treasure chest. "Guys, I think Steve, Lucy, and Max are trying to figure out what is causing the storm and if they can stop it."

"Maybe the chest is modded," suggested Emma, "which is why Steve is there."

The girls crowded around the window and watched as Steve buried the treasure chest.

"Should we go down there and ask them if they need any help?" Mia asked. "We never got to work on the farm this morning, and we have a while before dinner."

"Good idea," Julia said. She wanted to know what was happening with the chest and if somehow they had unleashed something awful onto the school. She truly hoped that this wasn't the case, but if it was, she was going to do something to stop it.

The trio spotted Cayla on the stairs. "Do we have class?" Cayla asked.

"No, we're just going to volunteer on the school farm," Julia replied.

"I love farming," Cayla said. "Do you think they'd mind if I came along?"

"Well . . ." Julia paused.

"No," Mia said. "I'm sure Steve would love the help."

"Lucy told me about the farm," Cayla said. "I actually got into the school for farming."

"There's another student, Nick, who is a farmer and volunteers on the farm," Emma said.

Julia couldn't understand how her friends could be so casual after what had happened with the treasure chest.

How could they forget to mention the treasure chest to Cayla?

"I see you've met Cayla. She is a great farmer," said Steve, who had just looked up to see the group approaching.

Mia said, "We wanted to help out on the farm. We hope that's okay."

"Of course." Steve picked a shovel from his inventory. "We should focus on a different section of the farm."

"That makes sense," Julia said, "after everything that happened this morning."

"What happened?" Cayla asked.

Before anyone had a chance to respond, Julia's shovel hit a hard surface deep underneath the dirt. "I think there's something here."

Steve looked into the hole and used his shovel to remove the excess dirt. He jumped into the hole and climbed up, holding another treasure chest.

"A treasure chest!" Cayla screamed with excitement.

"Don't open it!" Julia shouted. She didn't want another potent rainstorm to overtake the campus, but didn't have the energy to explain all of the details to this new student.

"Why not?" Cayla looked confused. She knew this was a great find and wanted to see what treasures were in the chest. "I want to do it. You can't stop me."

Steve rushed over to Cayla, "No, please, don't. That isn't a normal treasure chest."

"How do you know?" questioned Cayla.

"We had an incident earlier with a treasure chest that we found on the farm. Please just stay away from it." Steve said.

"I'm sorry," Cayla said, looking down at the mysterious chest.

"There's no reason to apologize. We just have to be very careful," Steve said.

"What should we do?" Julia questioned.

"Nothing at the moment," Steve replied as he moved between them and the chest.

The group noticed Lucy and Max walking toward them. Steve called out to them, "We found another one."

Chapter 5
ZOMBIE STRIKE

"Open it," Lucy instructed.

"What? No!" Julia didn't even realize the words shot out of her mouth. She didn't want to defy Lucy, but she was afraid that opening the chest would create another storm. She quickly grabbed a potion from her inventory and took a sip. She wasn't going into a battle unprepared.

"Julia," Lucy said calmly. "I know you're nervous because of the battle earlier today, but we have to open this chest. We might encounter hostile mobs and other threats once we open it, but we don't have a choice. We need to figure out what's going on, so the only choice is to be brave."

Julia knew Lucy was right, but that didn't erase the fact that she was petrified. "Can I have a minute to put on my armor?"

"That's a good idea," Lucy said.

Cayla was utterly confused. She was new and didn't know how much trouble could be in store. "What exactly happened earlier? I don't understand what you're talking about at all."

Emma explained what had happened when they found the chest earlier that day. Cayla gasped.

"Open it, Steve." Max leaned over the chest.

Steve opened the chest. "Emeralds."

"It's safe. It's not raining." Cayla looked up at the sky.

"Not quite." Steve lifted an emerald from the chest and the sky grew dark, and a lightning bolt struck the flagpole on the great lawn. Rain soaked the campus, and two zombies lumbered toward the group.

"Put it back," Lucy ordered as she clutched her diamond sword.

Steve carefully placed the emerald back in the chest as the sun came out. "There has to be curse on this chest."

"I don't believe in curses." Max inspected the chest.

"It doesn't matter if you believe in curses," replied Lucy. "I think someone doesn't want us to take anything from the chest, and they are hiding their treasures on the campus."

"These chests could be all over the campus," Steve said.

"Yes," Lucy added. "They could even have been here before the school was built. We have no idea."

The sky turned dark and another lightning bolt lit up the campus. Skeletons and zombies spawned from all directions. Julia gripped her sword tightly as she asked, "Steve, are you sure everything is back in the chest?"

Steve opened the chest and counted the emeralds. Four skeletons surprised him and he didn't have time to fight back. He was struck with a multitude of arrows that pierced his unarmored limbs, destroying him.

"Steve!" Lucy cried as she engaged in her own zombie battle. Four vacant-eyed zombies reeking of rotten flesh surrounded her. Lucy held her breath to avoid taking in any of the horrible odor as she slayed the undead beasts.

Zombies and skeletons cornered Julia, and her sword wasn't powerful enough to fight them. She cried out for Emma, but her friend was nowhere in sight. Mia and Cayla were busy battling a cluster of zombies, and Lucy and Max were engaged in a battle against a skeleton army. Julia was on her own, and she was having a hard time trying to battle the tricky mobs.

Julia had only been able to take a quick sip of the potion before the battle began, so her energy bar was incredibly low. She barely had the energy to swing her sword or grab another sip of potion from her inventory so that she could regain her strength or call for help. The last thing she saw were two green zombie arms reach for her and the horrid smell of rotten flesh. It was over.

* * * *

"Emma." Julia looked over as she respawned in her bed. Emma was standing by the window, watching the battle.

"I'm sorry," Emma said quietly. "I just can't do it."

Julia said, "You know we can't do it alone. The campus is in under attack and you're the only one who can help us."

"Find someone else," Emma responded in a monotone voice as she continued to watch the battle from the comfort of their dorm room.

"But we need your help," Julia said as she sipped a potion of strength. "I have to go back and help them. Will you come with me?"

"I can't. I really can't," Emma repeated.

"Is this about the Olympics?" Julia asked.

A thunderous noise shook the window, Emma covered her ears. "I asked you to leave me alone," she begged.

"What's the worst thing that can happen? If you get destroyed battling the skeletons and zombies, you'll respawn back here. Is that so bad?"

"It's not that," Emma replied.

"Then what is it?"

There was no time for Emma's reply. Two zombies ripped their door from its hinges and lunged toward them. Julia pierced one of the zombies with her sword, weakening the beast. She swiftly pulled a potion from her inventory, splashing it on the creature of the night. The splash was enough to annihilate one zombie while she battled with the stronger, second zombie.

Emma stood by the window watching the battle. Julia cried out for help, but she didn't move from her spot. Julia delivered a final blow, obliterating the zombie and ending the battle.

"Emma!" Julia was annoyed. "Don't make me battle these beasts alone."

"I want to help," Emma confessed, "but when I see them, I become paralyzed with fear."

"I know how you feel," Julia said. "That was the way I reacted before I met you. There's hope. You will overcome this fear. I did."

"How?" Emma asked.

"It's not easy," Julia said, "but you just have to try. Once you start fighting, you'll realize that it's not that hard."

As Julia spoke, four skeletons rushed into their room, aiming their bows at the girls. Julia fearlessly raced toward them, striking two with her sword. Five zombies walked behind the skeletons. They were outnumbered. Julia panicked. She needed Emma to help her, or they'd both be destroyed.

"Please, Emma." Julia pleaded, but there was no response. Julia tried to battle the mobs on her own, but her energy was fading fast. She used everything in her inventory to annihilate the mobs in the center of her room, but the battle was overwhelming her. Julia was ready to surrender.

She called out one final time, "Emma, you're the only person I know who could win this battle."

Julia was shocked to see Emma grab her potions and splash them on the skeletons and zombies, skillfully destroying them one by one.

Emma wore a wide-mouthed grin. "We did it."

"No, you did it," Julia said as the sun came out.

Mia, out of breath, rushed through the door with Cayla. "I can't believe what's happening."

"Me either." Julia smiled.

"Why are you smiling?" Mia asked.

"We had our own victory here." Julia looked over at Emma.

"Did you fight?" Mia sprinted over to Emma.

"Yes."

"Don't be modest. She singlehandedly destroyed a bunch of skeletons and zombies," Julia bragged about her friend.

Cayla changed the subject to announce, "I think I know why all of this is happening. I have some information about the chests."

Chapter 6
A QUESTION OF TRUST

"What?" Julia asked.

"I'm not sure if it's anything," Cayla said, "but my family has a long history at this school. I remember my mom telling me a story about secret treasure buried on campus, and how if it was ever found, bad things would happen."

"Really?" Emma questioned. "What type of bad things?"

Mia asked, "Like these storms?"

"Even worse," Cayla said.

"Even worse?" Julia repeated. What could be worse than what was happening?

"But you know it is a story that has been passed down, and stories like that tend to grow as they are being told. People embellish and we never know what is fact and fiction," Cayla said.

"I bet Aaron would know something about this," Mia said. "He was a student here years ago. If this story is a part of the campus folklore, he might have more information."

"Good thinking," Emma said.

Julia looked at the clock. "We have to go to dinner. It's almost over. We don't want to miss it."

The dining hall was crowded, and Julia heard even more crazy tales about the afternoon battle as she walked through the dining hall.

"I think those farm volunteers are behind these attacks."

"We thought they were destroyed."

"They were, but they came back."

"They have special powers and want to take over the campus."

"We don't trust them."

Julia sprinted back to the table, her body shaking. "I'm really worried, because I keep hearing snippets of conversations, and it appears that some students think we're behind these attacks."

"How?" Emma asked.

"Why?" Mia was appalled.

"But I just got here," Cayla explained. "Am I included in this?"

"I don't know," Julia's voice cracked. "I hope the students don't turn against us. That would be awful."

It was too late. Three girls wearing matching red berets walked over to them. One of the bereted girls threw a piece of chicken and screamed, "Stop terrorizing our school!"

"But we're not. We want to help the school." Julia could barely get the words out.

Mia clutched a potion in self-defense as the girl shouted and pointed to Mia's bottle. "Look, she's ready to attack us!"

"I only took it out because you threw chicken at us," Mia defended us.

"We're watching you," the girl said, and walked away with her two friends trailing behind her.

Julia sighed. "This is going to be harder than we thought."

"We have to find Aaron. He can help us." Mia quickly ate her beef and potatoes.

Julia agreed. "He can, but we have to be careful. We don't want to attract any more attention to ourselves. We don't want to be attacked by any of the students."

"I have no idea why they think we're behind this." Emma was annoyed.

The group exited the dining hall as everyone turned around and glared at them. Whispers could be heard throughout the dining hall.

"This feels awful," Emma said to her friends.

"I know. We have to clear our names," Mia said.

"And save the school," Julia added.

"Let's first find Aaron," Emma said as they walked out of the dining hall and toward the faculty houses.

The light was on in Aaron's room. His room was on the ground floor and was sparsely decorated. Aaron didn't like to spend a lot of time on campus. Although he enjoyed working at the school, he preferred to spend most of his free time in the stronghold, where he'd brew his potions. As they entered the building, Julia spotted Lucy walking down the hall.

"What are you guys doing in the faculty houses?" Lucy asked.

"Cayla mentioned that she heard a story about the treasure chest, and we wanted to confirm it with Aaron," Julia explained.

Cayla told Lucy about the story she had heard from her mother, who had attended this school years before.

"Interesting," Lucy said. "I've never heard about this. I wonder if Aaron has." Lucy knocked on Aaron's door.

Aaron was dressed in dyed blue armor and a green helmet. "Excuse me. I didn't think I was going to have any visitors."

"Sorry to bother you," Lucy said, "but—"

Aaron interrupted, "I just want to explain why I'm dressed like this. I often wear this when I'm brewing potions. It inspires me."

"That's wonderful," Mia said. "I wear a cap when I brew potions."

Aaron laughed. "I guess I'm not the only one who likes to get dressed up when they work."

Lucy wasn't there to discuss work habits; she wanted to get any information Aaron had about the treasure chest. "Aaron, we have a question about a treasure chest."

Lucy then asked Cayla to tell Aaron all she knew. Cayla repeated the story. "Have you heard about this cursed treasure chest?"

"No. Either that was before my time or after it. But it's strange that I never heard anything about it. Stories like that usually stick around," Aaron said.

"Maybe I should go home and ask my family," Cayla suggested.

"Maybe we should go with you," Julia said. "The entire school thinks we're the ones behind the attacks and are talking about us."

"Yes," Emma added. "Everyone was talking about us in the cafeteria. It was awful."

"I don't think you need to leave the campus. If we close the chest and don't remove the treasures, things remain peaceful," Lucy said. "From now on, we won't tempt fate, and we will leave the chests closed. I will hold an assembly to explain what happened. This will stop the students from focusing on you guys and will end these awful rumors. I'm sorry you have to deal with this."

"I think holding an assembly is a great idea," Julia exclaimed. "Once everyone knows the facts, life will go back to normal."

Aaron pointed toward the window. "It's getting dark out there. You guys should head home."

"I will announce the assembly at breakfast," Lucy told them.

Julia was thrilled as they walked across the great lawn toward their dorms. The girls were steps from their room when Cayla shrieked in pain. They turned around to see a spider's red-eyed menacing stare. A Spider Jockey was just inches from them.

Chapter 7
ANNOUNCEMENTS

Mia's arrow was the first one to hit the Spider Jockey, scraping the side of the black spider. She aimed and shot another arrow. The impact from the second arrow shook the spider, forcing the skeleton off the red-eyed spider. Cayla leapt at the falling skeleton, slamming her sword into its bony frame. Emma grabbed a potion from her inventory, splashing the skeleton, while Cayla delivered the final blow, destroying the bony beast.

"Pick up the dropped bone," Julia called out as she battled the spider. She tried not to get scared as she stared into its red glowing eyes. With four blows from her sword, she slayed the powerful eight-legged beast.

"We have to get back to our rooms," Mia called out to the others. The girls raced inside the building as they kept a close eye for any hostile mobs that might be spawning in the dimly lit halls.

Julia rushed into her bed and pulled the blue wool covers over herself. She was exhausted, and hoped everything would be cleared up the next day and the other students wouldn't torment them. She fell asleep with dreams about the assembly and having her name cleared.

* * * *

The next morning, Julia rubbed her eyes and saw Emma staring out the window.

"Is everything okay?" Julia asked.

"Yes." Emma looked at the sun flooding the lush, green campus. "I don't know if I'm in the mood for breakfast."

"Really?" Mia asked.

"I don't want to go into the dining hall, where everyone will stare," Emma explained.

"I know how you feel, but we can't let them bother us," Mia said.

"If we don't go, we'll appear guilty," Julia said, "and once breakfast is over, the whole school will feel badly for tormenting us."

Cayla stood by the door. "Are you guys going to breakfast?"

Yes," Julia replied. "We were just about to go. But are you sure you want to be seen with us?"

"Yes," Cayla laughed. "I know you guys weren't behind these attacks. I will be happy to defend you."

Emma reluctantly joined the others at breakfast. As they all expected, once they entered the dining hall, they were met by intense glares and whispers. Julia wanted to hide behind her tray, but instead she strode confidently through the dining hall. She didn't want anyone knowing how upset she was, as again she heard snippets of conversations.

"Lucy should have them removed from the campus."

"They're probably staging all of this because they failed to win the Minecraft Academic Olympics."

"I can't wait until they're in the bedrock jail with Hallie. I'll feel so much safer."

Julia tried not to let these comments sting, but that was a nearly impossible feat. She just wanted life to go back to normal.

The gang ate their breakfast in silence. They were too busy listening to the hum of gossip to start a conversation with each other. Brad walked over to their table, breaking their silence. "Are you guys ready for Henry's survival class today? I hear he's taking us to the Nether."

"All I hear is people talking about how awful we are," Julia said. "I haven't been paying attention to school."

"Well, you should pay attention to schoolwork. Today, we're going to learn important skills to use in the Nether. I really dislike that place, so I'm glad I can get some tips." Brad smiled.

Julia turned to hear Lucy's announcement. She stood in the center of the dining hall and addressed the students. "After breakfast, there is an assembly in the Great Hall. Please meet me there as soon as you finish eating."

When Lucy exited, the entire dining hall gazed at their table. Julia gulped. "I bet they all think we're going to be punished in front of the school."

Brad said, "Don't waste your time worrying about what these people think. You know you're innocent and so does Lucy."

"I guess you're right," Julia said, "but it still hurts to have the entire school talking about you and staring at you."

"Or throwing chicken at you," added Emma.

Julia announced that she wasn't in the mood to eat anymore and the others agreed, they exited the dining hall, and were one of the first people to arrive at the assembly. Lucy called out to them, "Julia, Emma, and Mia, please come to the podium. I want you to stand by me as I make my announcement."

The trio stood next to Lucy as students crowded into the auditorium in the Great Hall. Lucy started to speak.

"I'm gathering you all here to address an incident that happened yesterday. I know there are many rumors circulating around campus, but what I will tell you are the facts. Our visiting faculty member Steve, who is also an expert farmer, was creating a farm on campus with some volunteers. While he was working on the farm, he found a chest. He opened the chest and took out a diamond. Once he removed the diamond, it began to rain. However, once he placed the diamond back, the rain ceased. This happened again when he discovered a second chest later that day. We aren't sure if these chests were cursed, but we do know that if we leave them alone, we are fine. We will work tirelessly to find out who placed the chests on the campus and why we can't remove these treasures, but you must be patient."

Students raised their hands. Lucy said, "I can only take a few questions."

A girl with green hair asked, "Are there any students who might be behind the attack?"

"As you can see, I have a few of the student volunteers with me. These innocent students were accused of being the culprits behind these attacks and have suffered viciously from the fellow students at this school. I truly expected more from the students at such a prestigious academy. Please leave these three girls alone and let them study in peace. They have done nothing wrong, and have only helped the school by volunteering to build a farm on campus."

The assembly was over and the gang rushed to Henry's survival class. Henry asked the students if anybody knew how to build a portal to the Nether. Emma whispered to Julia, "Wow, that's so basic."

Julia didn't reply. She still had to look up how to craft a portal to the Nether. Brad raised his hand and started to rattle off the list of ingredients for crafting a portal to the Nether, when a loud boom shook the small classroom.

"What was that?" Brad asked.

"It sounds like thunder," Henry said as he pulled his armor from his inventory and instructed the class to do the same.

Julia grabbed her armor. As she put it on, she saw a group of students whispering and staring at her.

"Oh, no!" a student gasped as a rare skeleton horseman rode past the classroom window.

Julia shivered as she clutched her sword. She wasn't sure if she would have to battle the other students or the skeleton horseman.

Chapter 8
LOOTED

Boom!

The ear-shattering thunder rattled the classroom as Julia sprinted toward the bony horse and the skeleton riding atop of it. The skeleton horse's legs clanged as it raced around the campus. A flash of lightning shot across the campus, and Julia narrowly avoided being struck as she caught up with the horse. Julia leapt at the skeleton horse, but it sprinted away without a scratch.

"What's going on?" Mia called out in utter horror.

The campus lawn filled with zombies, skeletons, creepers, and Endermen.

"This is going to be an epic battle," Brad said as he struck a zombie with his sword. "I'm glad we have Henry by our side."

Henry showed off his survival skills as zombies, skeletons, and a creeper surrounded him. Using a mixture of potions and his enchanted diamond sword, Henry fought off the evil mobs that cornered him by the classroom entrance.

Kaboom!

"That didn't sound like thunder!" Julia exclaimed as a loud explosion rocked the campus. Smoke rose through the sky, clouding Julia's vision, and she didn't see three skeletons lunge toward her as one of the bony beasts delivered its final blow. Julia awoke in her bed and raced to the window.

The campus was under attack. Every hostile mob of the Overworld battled the student body under rainy skies. Students slipped on the soggy grass as they raced toward skeletons and zombies. Julia spotted Mia splashing through a puddle as she sprinted from a skeleton army that trailed closely behind her. Julia knew she had to help her friends. She rushed from the dorm and raced back into the thick of the rainy battle.

"Help!" Cayla cried as three green creepers detonated in front of her. Julia caught a glimpse of Cayla before she was destroyed.

Julia spotted Lucy in the middle of an intense zombie battle and rushed to her side. "Did someone find another treasure chest?"

"Not that I know of." Lucy could barely spit the words out as she struggled to destroy the new crop of zombies that spawned in front of her. "Do you know what was destroyed in the explosion?"

Julia hadn't seen anything but smoke. "No," she replied as she slayed a zombie. "Hopefully there was no damage."

Lucy gasped as six more zombies lumbered toward them. As she reached for a potion of strength, the sun came out, and she let out a sigh of relief. "We have to find out what exploded."

Julia and Lucy didn't have to travel very far to investigate the explosion. Brad ran over to them, and in one breath he said, "The dining hall. Someone blew up the dining hall."

Henry sprinted over. "Brad, we don't know if someone blew it up. It might have been struck by lightning and caught fire."

Lucy took a deep breath. "I am going to hope this storm was just a natural occurrence in the Overworld and that the school is not under another attack."

"We should go investigate the dining hall. I didn't find any TNT, but we have to be sure there wasn't something else that caused the fire," Henry said.

Julia looked up at the sunny sky as she walked across the campus. It was shocking to see how much of a difference the sun made. When clouds obscured the sun or it was nighttime, you were incredibly vulnerable in the Overworld. As the sun's rays beat down on Julia, she felt a sense of calm, but this inner peace was quickly shattered when Emma and Mia raced toward them. "We found another chest," Emma called out.

"What?" Lucy asked. "Where?"

Emma reached them. "It was on the floor of the dining hall."

"Is the dining hall badly damaged?" Henry asked.

"No, not too bad," Mia said. "It was a small explosion. I couldn't find any TNT, so I'm not sure how it was started."

"I couldn't find any either," Brad said.

Emma led the gang toward the empty chest. Julia looked at the gaping hole on the side of the dining hall. "That isn't too hard to repair. I can fix it if you'd like," she offered.

"Yes." Lucy was happy to have the help. "That would be fantastic."

"I'd also like to help," Brad added.

"Of course," Lucy said. "We want this repaired as quickly as possible."

The empty chest sat on the floor underneath one of the cafeteria tables. Julia leaned down and peered inside. "It's completely looted."

Lucy looked at the empty chest. "I guess this is what caused the storm."

"But why did the storm stop? Nobody replaced the items," Julia said.

"I don't know," Lucy replied as she stared at the empty chest, hoping to find an answer.

Cayla called out to them. "Guys, over here."

They sprinted toward Cayla, who stood by a table near the kitchen. As they reached Cayla, they spotted a chest by her feet.

"Another chest," Henry said as he reached over and opened it. The chest was overflowing with diamonds and emeralds.

"I wonder if someone placed the loot from the empty chest into this one, and that stopped the storm," Julia theorized.

"I'm not sure." Lucy looked through the chest and picked up a diamond, which instantly set off a thunderous sound.

"Put it back," Emma begged.

Lucy quickly replaced the diamond, and the storm ended before it even began. Lucy looked up at Cayla. "I think you're going to have to return home. We need to know what information your family has about these chests."

"But it could just be some crazy tale," Cayla said.

"Sometimes there is truth in those stories. Also, we have no other leads." Lucy instructed Cayla, "I think you should bring Julia, Mia, Emma, and Brad with you. With all that is happening on campus, I think it's safer if you travel with a group."

"When do you want us to leave?" Cayla asked.

"As soon as possible."

"Where do you live?" Brad asked.

"Mushroom Island," Cayla said.

"I've never been there," Brad said. "I hear it's gorgeous."

"Brad, this isn't a vacation," Lucy reminded him. "We need you to travel there and get any information you can to help us solve this problem."

"We understand," Cayla said. "We'll report back on everything we find."

Henry instructed them to search through their inventories to make sure they had everything they needed for their trip.

"I can probably use a few more potions," Cayla said.

Mia said, “Don’t worry. I have enough for everyone.”

As the gang exited the campus, Julia could see the three girls in berets standing on the great lawn. They stared at her. Julia wanted to call out, letting them know she wasn’t a criminal. She wanted to let them know that she was hopefully going to save the campus.

Chapter 9
JOURNEY TO MUSHROOM ISLAND

"How much further?" Mia questioned.

Cayla pulled out a map and showed it to the group. "We have to go through the cold biome and over a mountain until we reach the shore, where we'll have to construct boats to get us to Mushroom Island," she explained.

"The cold biome," Julia repeated, excited to get there. It had been too long since she'd been in the familiar icy biome. She missed snow and building igloos.

"Yes," said Cayla. "Maybe you can construct an igloo for us."

"That would be great. I'd love to do that," Julia exclaimed.

Julia could see the white snow in the distance and her heart raced with excitement. This wasn't the cold biome that she had grown up in, but it was still extremely familiar. She raced toward the snowy landscape with her friends following her. Even though Julia knew the trip wasn't a vacation, she was still happy to be traveling alongside her friends. Julia was the first person to reach the cold biome. As she stepped on the ice, she reached over and picked up a patch of snow, slowly and carefully crafting a snowball.

"Watch out!" She giggled as she threw the snowball at her friends.

Emma, Mia, Cayla, and Brad quickly grabbed snow and made their own snowballs. Soon the group was laughing as snowballs shot through the air. Julia loved feeling the fresh cold snow against her skin. The wet snow fell down her cheek, and Julia laughed as she ducked from the sea of snowballs that were flying at her.

"Time out," she hollered as she looked up at the sky. "It's getting dark. I should build the igloo now. We don't want to waste our time fighting hostile mobs. We need to get some sleep before our trip tomorrow."

"You're only saying that because you're being pelted with snowballs," Brad said as he threw another snowball at Julia.

"No." Julia smiled. "I wish we could have a longer snowball fight, but I think we have to stay focused."

"I know what you mean," Cayla said. "There is something fun about this trip. It feels like a vacation."

The rest of the gang agreed this was a fun trip, but there was also a purpose to the trip. If they could get information about the chests, they could help the school.

Julia thought about the explosion in the dining hall as she crafted the foundation for igloo.

Brad worked alongside Julia. "When I worked on the igloo this summer, I stayed in another one that had a trapdoor underneath the carpet."

"Yes, that is usually found in naturally generated igloos. I'd put one in here, but since we're only staying here for the night, our igloo is going to be a bit simpler." Julia placed a brick of snow to build the side of the igloo. "What did you find in the trapdoor?"

"It was super cool. I found a chest with golden apples."

"Wow, that's cool." Julia worked with Brad to complete the igloo.

Cayla breathlessly rushed over to them. "I saw something." She tried to catch her breath.

"What?" Julia asked.

Emma also sprinted over and caught her breath. "Guys, I saw a polar bear."

"If you stay away from the polar bear, it won't bother you," Julia explained. "Is that what you saw, Cayla?"

"No," Cayla said. "I saw a person."

"Where?" asked Brad.

Cayla pointed toward a snow-covered mountain. "I could swear I saw a man in a purple jacket. When he saw me, he sprinted over the mountain."

Julia looked at the mountain. She didn't see any man wearing a purple jacket. "I think we should all keep a close eye on our surroundings. You never know who we'll encounter in this snowy biome."

Brad said, "I just finished the igloo. Do you guys want to help construct beds?"

"Yes," Julia said. "We have to get ready for the night. We have a long day ahead of us tomorrow."

As they entered the igloo, Cayla marveled at what a great job they had done. "You guys created such a homey igloo."

Emma added, "I can't believe you built this so quickly."

Mia agreed and then asked, "Can I craft my bed by the window?"

"Yes," Julia said.

The gang worked on their beds as night was setting in. Mia gasped as a polar bear walked past the window. "I know they aren't going to hurt me, but they are scary, right? I mean, they're enormous."

"They do take some getting used to," Julia said.

The group got into their beds. Cayla called out, "Tomorrow we head to the shore. We just have to get over that mountain."

"I'm afraid of heights," Brad confessed.

"We will be with you," Julia said. "You'll be okay. We'll take it very slowly."

Mia sat up in bed and shrieked.

"Is there another polar bear walking past your window?" Julia asked.

"No." Mia quivered. "I think there's someone outside."

Chapter 10
SNOWBALLS AND SHELTER

Emma lit her torch, opened the door, and slipped on the icy ground.

Julia rushed over to her side. "Are you okay?"

"Yes." Emma stood up. "I didn't realize it would be that slippery."

"Do you see anybody?" asked Mia.

"I don't see anyone." Julia placed a torch on the side of the igloo and looked out at the snowy mountainous biome covered with fern trees and snow-capped mountains.

"What did the person look like?" Cayla asked.

"I'm not sure. He was too fast," Mia said as she stood by the entrance to the igloo.

"Watch out," Brad hollered to Emma as a zombie walked toward her. Its arms extended in front of the undead creature as it reached for her.

Emma struck the zombie with her sword until it was destroyed. She picked up a piece of rotten flesh from the ground and placed it in her inventory. "Maybe you just saw a zombie," she said to Mia.

"No," Mia declared. "I know what I saw and it was a person. I think he was wearing a purple coat."

"A purple coat?" Cayla questioned. "I saw someone with a purple coat climbing up the mountain."

"We have to find him," Mia said as she readjusted her armor and prepared for battle.

"I don't think searching for someone in the middle of the night is the best idea," Brad said. "I think we should get some sleep."

"I agree," said Julia. "We don't know if this person is evil. It could just be someone who lives in the biome."

The group was torn. Mia and Cayla wanted to find out who was lurking by their house in the middle of the night, but Emma, Julia, and Brad wanted to sleep. They decided to take a vote, and since it was three to two, they wound up heading back into the igloo for the night.

Mia looked out the window before she went to bed, but there was nothing there, not even a polar bear. She quietly said, "Good night."

* * * *

Julia was the first to wake up in the morning, and she spotted a polar bear walking past the window. She opened the door, ready to spend some quiet time alone in the snowy biome. Julia wanted to watch the polar bear peacefully walk through the snow-filled landscape. She sprinted out the door and fell over something, letting out a cry.

"Julia?" Emma called out.

"Are you hurt?" Brad asked.

"No, I'm fine," Julia said as she brushed snow off her leg. "But you guys should come out here and see what I've found."

The gang rushed toward the door. Emma looked down. "A chest?"

Mia said, "I told you someone was outside the window last night. I bet they left the chest here."

Julia opened the chest. "Wow, golden apples." She looked at the chest filled with enchanted, glistening apples.

Mia leaned over and pulled one out. Julia screamed, "What are you doing?"

"This is an experiment," she said as she clutched the apple.

"Nothing is happening," Julia said. "I guess that's a good sign."

Snow started to fall. "You spoke too soon," Mia said as she placed the golden apple back in the chest and the snow stopped.

"Pick it up again," Julia instructed.

Mia grabbed a golden apple. As she pulled it from the chest, a brisk wind was felt in the air and snow fell hard against the icy ground. Mia quickly put it back, and the storm ended.

"I think this is some kind of message. They want us to leave them alone," Mia said.

"It could be," Julia said, "but this isn't going to stop us from finding out who is behind all of this."

Cayla cried out, "Look!"

A man in a purple jacket sprinted away in the distance. His colorful jacket stuck out against the stark white snow as he started to climb the mountain.

"We have to follow him," Julia said.

The gang put on their armor as they sprinted toward the man. Julia sipped a potion of swiftness to help her speed up. "Stop," she called out.

The man ran faster, but Julia caught up to him. She splashed a potion of weakness on him, and he stopped.

"What do you want from me?" he asked, his voice very weak.

"I have the same question for you," Julia said as her friends surrounded the man in the purple jacket.

"Who are you?" Brad asked.

"Did you leave that chest?" Mia asked.

"Are you the one who planted chests on Minecrafters Academy?" Cayla asked.

"What's your problem?" Emma asked.

"So many questions," the man replied. "And I'm not answering any of them." He disappeared.

"He must have TPed somewhere and to someone," Brad said.

"But where?" Julia asked. She looked around the snowy biome, but he was nowhere to be found.

Chapter 11
DEEP BELOW THE SEA

"I'm sure we'll find him," Emma said as the group made their way up the mountain.

"I agree. I bet that's not the last we'll see of him," said Brad, looking down as he took each step. Julia stood by him, making sure he wasn't scared.

Cayla stopped at the top of the mountain, but Julia urged her to keep going. "No," Cayla insisted. "Brad, I know you're scared, but I just want you to see this view. It's incredible."

Emma gawked at the view. In the distance they could see the shoreline. "Cayla's right. You shouldn't miss out on this view because you're scared. When I started school, I was afraid to battle."

"Really?" Brad asked.

"Yes," Emma confessed. "After losing the Minecrafters Academic Olympics, I thought I'd never be able to battle again."

"How did you get back to fighting?" Brad asked as he stood close to Julia and away from the mountain's peak.

"With the help of my friends." Emma smiled at Julia. "And I want to help you. Just walk over to me. Once you do, you'll see the most stunning sight ever."

Brad reluctantly walked over to Emma as Julia stayed close to his side. He looked out at the panoramic view of the Overworld. He could see the ocean and the forest. "Wow, this is gorgeous. I've never seen such a beautiful view."

"See? I told you it was worth it," Emma said as she helped Brad make his way down the mountain and toward the grassy biome.

Cayla studied the map. "We're almost at the shoreline."

"I can build the boats," Brad said.

"I can help you," Julia said.

"Great," Cayla said, and then paused.

"What's the matter?" Julia asked.

"I thought I saw that man again." She stared at trees ahead, but she didn't see him.

"I wonder who he is," Emma said.

"I have a bad feeling about him," Julia told them.

"We can't focus on that man," Cayla said. "We have to get to the shore and craft the boats."

The group hurried toward the shore. Once they reached the beach, everyone gathered wooden planks from their inventories and handed them to Brad and Julia. The duo diligently crafted the boats.

"Wow, these are really nice," Cayla said as she eyed the first boat. It was simple and small in design, but sturdy and compact. Cayla pulled the boat onto the calm blue water.

Julia constructed the last boat and as she placed it in the water, she noticed an icy patch in the distance. "I worry the icy conditions of the water might crash the boat."

Cayla reassured her, "We can break the ice with the boat. We'll be fine. When you grow up on an island, you become an expert on boating. If I didn't know how to navigate the seas, I'd never get off the island."

The boat ride wasn't very long, and within a few minutes of floating on the peaceful sea, Emma spotted land. "I see a large mushroom. It's prettier than I imagined. I can't wait to see Mushroom Island. I want a bowl of Mooshroom Stew."

"Remember," Cayla told her, "we have a job to do."

"I know," Emma said, "but Mooshroom Stew is so good and really hard to come by in the Overworld. Besides, if we don't eat, we won't have any energy."

The conversation was cut short as the current grew stronger and the boats picked up speed. The rough waters challenged the boaters as each of them grasped onto the side of boat, hoping they wouldn't be tossed overboard by the extremely forceful current.

"Hang on," Cayla said. "We're almost there."

"I'm trying," Mia said as she clutched the side of the boat.

Julia's boat shook violently, and hit a rock. The boat was demolished and Julia was alone in the deep blue water. "Help!" Julia cried as she was dragged underneath the sea. Julia swam to the surface as her friends tried to lead their boats toward her, but the current was too powerful, and her friends drifted further away. Julia grabbed a potion of water breathing and took a large gulp as she was pulled underneath the deep blue ocean.

Underneath the water, Julia could see the bottom of one of the wooden boats and tried to swim to the surface, but a squid got in her way, and by the time she reached the surface, the boat was gone. She looked in every direction, but she couldn't find her friends. She was lost at sea. The sea was still rough, and Julia knew it was safer to be underneath the water. As she swam deep down toward the ocean's graveled ground, she spotted an ocean monument. Julia grabbed her arm as she felt a pain radiate down the side, and turned around to see a guardian's tail moving swiftly. The turquoise fish with orange spikes shot lasers as it swam toward her.

Julia's health was dangerously low as she grabbed her bow and arrow and aimed for the hostile fish. As she swam closer to the fish, she grabbed her sword and slammed it into the guardian, and was relieved when the fish was destroyed. She swam toward the ocean monument, but there were three guardians swimming by the entrance, and Julia knew she had to come up with a quick plan to enter the ocean monument. Julia grabbed a potion of strength from her inventory and took a sip as she swam toward the guardians with a sword in her hand.

The sword pierced one guardian as the other two shot lasers. She took a deep breath as she tried to conserve her energy, and she plunged the sword into the guardian for a second time, destroying the fish. She followed the same plan with the other guardian, annihilating them, and then quickly sipped a potion of healing to replenish her energy. Even Julia was shocked when she singlehandedly destroyed the three fish and picked up the prismarine crystals the guardian dropped.

She knew ocean monuments contained treasures like gold bricks, and she swam through the underwater castle in search of whatever treasure she might find. Julia turned around when she heard a familiar voice, but she couldn't see anyone.

"Julia!" a voice called out. "Over here."

Julia swam toward the sound of the voice, and spotted Cayla hiding behind a pillar from an elder guardian. She swam toward her, but the elder guardian spotted Julia and focused its powerful laser at her. She fearlessly swam toward the elder guardian with her sword and ripped into the protector of the ocean monument. Cayla joined Julia in the battle as they worked together to destroy the fish.

When the fish was annihilated and they were no longer threatened, Julia and Cayla swam toward the treasure chamber. They searched throughout the chamber but didn't find any treasure.

"Where are all of the gold bars?" Julia asked.

"I bet that man took them," Cayla said.

"We can't blame him for everything," Julia said.

"Let's get out of here. We have to find the others." Cayla swam out of the ocean monument and Julia followed.

Chapter 12
FAMILY TIES

"I don't see anyone," Julia said as she reached the surface.

"I see Mushroom Island!" Cayla exclaimed.

The two swam toward the island. As they reached land, they could see their friends sitting on a dock.

Julia and Cayla climbed onto the land as water dripped off them. Emma said, "We were looking all over for you guys. We were very worried."

"We were in an ocean monument," Cayla explained, "and it was looted."

"Incredible." Brad wanted to know all the details about the underwater monument, but Cayla was too focused on getting to her home.

"I live up that hill right behind that mushroom patch." Cayla pointed to a cluster of large red mushrooms.

The group followed Cayla, but Emma stopped them when she saw three mooshrooms strolling in a pasture.

"Can we milk them? Please. I am seriously craving Mushroom Stew."

"Yes," Cayla said. "Those are my neighbor's mooshrooms. They always let me milk them."

Cayla led them toward the mooshrooms, and she took out a bucket and leaned over and milked the red spotted cows. Emma was the first to drink the mushroom stew. "Tasty," Emma said as the others feasted on this local delicacy.

"Cayla," a voice called out.

"Mom!" Cayla smiled as she raced toward her mother.

Cayla's mother looked like her, with striking black hair. But her mother wasn't smiling, which Julia thought was odd. Wasn't she happy to be reunited with her daughter?

"There's trouble here," Cayla's mother told them. "You guys should leave. It isn't safe here."

"What are you talking about?" Cayla asked.

"There's someone here who is tormenting us. Our peaceful island is being attacked by some crazed person." Tears filled her mother's eyes. "I don't want you getting hurt."

"What does he look like?" Julia asked.

"He wears a purple jacket." Her mother wiped the tears from her eyes.

"We know who he is," Cayla said. "We think he's behind the attack at Minecrafters Academy."

"What's happening at the school? Are you guys okay?" Cayla's mother asked.

Cayla told her about the treasure chests and the storms. "We came back here to find out if you knew anything about these treasure chests. I remember you telling me a story about treasure chests on the campus."

"Yes." Her mom's eyes opened wide as she looked in each direction to ensure they were safe. "That happened right before I attended the school. There was a thief who buried treasure around campus."

"Did they ever find out who it was?" Cayla asked.

"No," her mother replied. "Truthfully, I thought it was just a rumor that my roommate started. My roommate would tell me stories about a thief who was at on an off-campus treasure hunt with other students. It was extremely successful, but while everyone was sleeping, the thief stole the chests from their closets. Nobody knew who it was. My roommate said she discovered a buried chest when she was farming. She tried to take out a diamond and it created a massive storm."

"That's what happened to us," Mia said. "It was awful."

"I wonder if the man in the purple jacket has anything to do with these treasure chests," Emma said.

"I don't know," said Cayla's mother. "But he has been here for two days and has staged many attacks across the island and scared the residents."

"Like what?" Brad asked.

"He summoned the Wither." Cayla's mother shook as she spoke.

"Wow," Cayla said and then screamed, "There he is!"

The man sprinted toward them. "You'd better leave those chests alone," he screamed, "or else!"

Julia leapt at the man, but he disappeared. "Did he have anybody with him?" Julia asked.

"Not that I saw," Cayla's mother said as she led them to her house. "I really think you guys are better off staying somewhere else, but I'll let you stay here because it seems like there is no safe place in the Overworld at the moment."

"We have to solve the mystery of these chests or the campus will remain under attack," Cayla said. "Do you remember anything else about the story?"

Cayla's mom shook her head. "That's all I remember. As I said, it was before my time. I think my roommate Karen would know more, but I've lost contact with her."

"We should track her down," Cayla suggested. "She might help us figure out who the thief is and what we can do to stop him."

"I don't even know where she could be. It was so long ago," her mom said as she entered her enormous mushroom house.

"This place is incredible." Julia marveled as she walked through the building, noticing the complicated design.

"Are you a builder?" Cayla's mom asked.

"Yes," Julia replied. "So is Brad."

"I'm a builder, too," Cayla's mom said.

"Did you build this house?" Julia asked.

"Yes." She showed them around the spacious home. Julia wanted to ask her a million questions about how she'd constructed the mushroom house, but there wasn't time to talk, because there was a loud deafening roar and a tail slammed through the roof, creating a gaping hole.

"Oh no!" Cayla cried. "The Ender Dragon!"

Chapter 13
LOOK UP

The muscular dragon circled in the air. The gang tried to shield themselves from the beast as they aimed their arrows at the dragon. Only one arrow pierced the side of the dragon. The sole arrow infuriated the dragon, and its fiery breath threw lethal fireballs at the group. The dragon focused its red eyes on Mia as it flew toward her at an incredibly close range. The dragon breathed, unleashing a fatal fireball and instantly annihilating Mia.

Julia teemed with anger as she used all her strength to plow her sword into the dragon's wing. The powerful dragon was surprised by the attack, and retaliated by spewing a potent fireball at Julia, but she sprinted from the fireball. Brad and Emma shot a barrage of arrows at the dragon, weakening it. Cayla and her mother struck the weakened dragon with their diamond swords until the beast exploded. A portal to the End formed in front of the mushroom house.

"Mia's gone," Julia said. "She must have respawned in the igloo."

"Hopefully she'll TP back here soon," Brad said.

Cayla's mom said, "We have to stop these attacks on Mushroom Island. This is a peaceful place."

"We have to find the man in the purple jacket," Brad said.

The group didn't have to search for the man. He suddenly appeared in front of them. "Help me," he gasped.

"What?" Julia was shocked.

Cayla aimed her arrow at the man.

"I'm not the one who is hurting you. I'm just the messenger," he pleaded. "I'm very weak and my inventory is empty. Does anybody have a potion of strength?"

"Why don't you just milk a mooshroom?" Cayla asked.

"I need something stronger," he begged. "If you lend me a potion, I will help you guys."

"Help us?" Brad was annoyed.

"Your dragon destroyed our alchemist, Mia. She was the one with all of the potions," Julia said.

Everyone was surprised when Cayla pulled a potion from her inventory and handed it to the man. He took a sip and thanked her. "I'm Johnny," he introduced himself to the group. "I need your help. Can you follow me?"

"Where?" Cayla asked.

"There's a cave," he explained, "where the person I'm working for is staying. It's where she keeps all her treasures. She's a—"

"A thief," Cayla's mom interrupted.

"She calls herself a treasure hunter," Johnny said.

"When you steal other people's treasures, I call you a thief," Cayla's mom said defiantly.

"You're right. She is a thief, and we have to stop her." Johnny pointed to the cave's entrance. "You have to come with me and stop her."

Julia paused outside the cave's entrance. "Why should we trust you? Maybe you'll trap us in the cave."

"There's five of you and one of me," Johnny reasoned.

"I don't trust you," Julia said.

Mia spawned in front of the cave's entrance. "He's telling the truth. There's someone else who is behind the treasure chests."

"Who?" Cayla questioned.

"When I spawned in the igloo, I saw woman with long red hair wearing a green dress. She was burying treasure. When I approached her, she asked me if the Ender Dragon destroyed me, and I asked her how she knew. She replied that she knew everything and that our campus was never going to be safe again."

"That's Karen. She's the one who is tormenting me," Johnny said. "She found me in a desert temple, where I was on my own treasure hunt. She told me if I helped her, she'd offer me countless diamonds. She said she needed help getting some old treasure back that she had buried."

"Karen. Red hair. That sounds like my old roommate at Minecrafters Academy," Cayla's mom said.

"Does she live in this cave?" Cayla asked.

"Yes," Johnny said, "but I guess she's in the icy biome now. Maybe we can find her there."

"How are we going to get back there?" Brad asked.

"I can teleport to her and you can come with me," Johnny suggested. "She has to be stopped, she has a bunch of plans under way that will jeopardize the entire Overworld."

"What if we just give her all of her treasure chests back? Will she leave us alone?" Julia asked.

"No, she wants more than her old chests. She said she didn't even remember burying them until someone found them and tried to take a diamond. When that happened, she was alerted that they were found. She has a bunch of other plans in action."

Johnny stopped talking when Karen appeared in front of them. "Talking about me?" she asked as she pointed her diamond sword against Johnny's chest.

Chapter 14
THE GREAT ESCAPE

"Karen!" Cayla's mom shouted. "It was you. You were the criminal."

"Yes." She laughed. "And you were the only person to whom I told that story, and I knew I had to come back here when I found out that your daughter was at Minecrafters Academy."

Cayla was the first to strike Karen. Karen dodged the blade as she hit Cayla with a diamond sword. The strike weakened Cayla, who fumbled with her sword as she tried to defend herself. Even with her friends by her side, Cayla lost the battle. Angered by Cayla's defeat, Julia struck Karen with all her might, puncturing Karen's unarmored body and destroying her.

"She'll spawn in her bed in the cave," Johnny told them.

The gang rushed into the cave, but Karen's bed was empty. "Where is she?" Julia asked.

"Maybe the icy biome?" Johnny suggested. "I have no idea."

Cayla spawned by the entrance to the cave and called to her friends, "Get out of the cave. I think Karen has TNT in there."

The group sprinted from the cave as it exploded behind them. Julia could barely see through the smoke-filled air. "Cayla, where's Karen?"

Cayla explained, "I saw Karen in the icy biome. She spawned in the bed next to me. I confronted her and she told me if I waited a few minutes I'd see all of my friends, and that she'd booby-trapped the cave."

"Where is she now?" Johnny asked.

"I don't know," Cayla replied. "She could be in the icy biome."

"I can't believe Karen is the same person I roomed with at school. I bet nobody knew she stole all of those treasures," Cayla's mom said.

"That's why Lucy and Aaron had never heard about this story. It was as if Karen was confessing only to you. It all makes sense now," Julia said.

"I never knew I was the only one she told this to," Cayla's mom said.

"We have to tell everyone on campus and warn them about Karen," Emma said. "She's probably heading there."

Brad suggested they TP to campus, and they all agreed. The group teleported back to campus, and as they emerged on the Great Lawn, they spawned in the middle of a rainy skeleton battle. Four skeletons aimed their bows at Julia. She tried to duck, but it was useless; she was outnumbered, and the four arrows weakened Julia until she had no hearts left and awoke in the igloo. Karen stood above her, holding a diamond sword at Julia's forehead.

"Why are you doing this?" Julia asked. "I'm sure the school would give you back all the treasure chests, even though you don't deserve them."

"They'd better," Karen said as she disappeared.

Julia teleported to Emma and Mia, who were in the middle of a battle with a zombie army that had viciously attacked them.

Lucy sprinted toward them and Julia called out, "Did someone take something out of the treasure chests? Why is it raining?"

"I don't think anybody took anything from the chests. All the students have been on high alert. We haven't let anyone dig into the ground," Lucy said as she struck a zombie with her diamond sword, and picked up the rotten flesh that dropped to the ground when the zombie was destroyed.

A lightning bolt flashed across the sky as the rain intensified and the campus flooded. A treasure chest rose from the dirt ground, and Julia raced toward it. She leaned over and opened the chest. "It's empty!"

"What?" Lucy rushed over to the chest. "How can this be?"

A new crop of zombies lumbered across the lawn and headed toward Julia and Lucy. They shot arrows to stop the undead beasts, but every time they destroyed one zombie, another spawned in its place. Zombies ripped the doors of the dorms and the other school buildings from their hinges.

Screams were heard throughout the campus. Julia looked at Lucy, "How are we going to stop this?"

"We will," Lucy said confidently.

Julia wanted to believe the headmistress could save the day, but she knew this wasn't an easy problem to solve. Julia weakened the zombies with the potion and then slayed them with her sword. She looked around and saw the entire campus battling all of the mobs of the Overworld. It seemed like a never-ending battle.

Brad was battling several skeletons, Emma and Mia were destroying tons of creepers, and Henry was in the midst of an intense zombie attack. Julia looked up at the sky, relieved that they didn't have to battle the Wither or the Ender Dragon. A skeleton's arrows struck her arm. She drank a potion to regain her strength and rushed toward the skeleton, slamming her sword against its bony frame. Lucy joined Julia in the battle.

Steve sprinted over to Julia and Lucy. As he helped them battle the skeletons, he said, "I found two empty chests."

"Oh no," Lucy said as she struck a skeleton.

In the middle of the rain, in the center of the campus, Karen spawned and grabbed an empty chest. She looked inside the empty chest and stood in the rain, hollering, "It won't stop raining until you come up with the treasure."

Chapter 15
THUNDEROUS THREATS

"Where is the treasure?" Julia cried as more skeletons spawned in the rain. Thunder boomed and lightning lit up the dark skies as more mobs spawned on the rainy campus.

"I'm drenched." Brad rubbed his eyes. Raindrops clouded his vision, which weakened his aim. The skeletons advanced toward Brad, and Julia tried to shield him from the arrows, but it was impossible and Brad was destroyed.

Julia wanted to find out who had stolen the treasure. She wondered if Karen had taken the treasures and was tricking everyone, but it was unlikely. Karen still stood in the center of the campus, threatening everyone. Her screams could be heard over the loud thunder.

"Whoever took my treasures must be found. If not, you will be cursed with an eternal rainstorm."

As Karen made this announcement, the rain stopped. She looked up at the sky as Julia rushed to her and said, "Maybe you aren't as powerful as you think."

"No," Karen said. "Somebody must have returned my treasure." She sprinted toward the Main Hall. Grabbing a shovel from her inventory, she began to dig into the wet ground. She pulled out a chest, opened it, and showed Julia its contents.

Julia was shocked to see the chest was filled with diamonds, "When did they do this?"

"I don't know," Karen said, "but it's all mine."

Lucy sprinted over to Karen. The rest of the faculty followed behind her. "You can't keep that treasure."

"You must be joking." Karen laughed at Lucy's comment.

"You're going to prison. You're a thief and you've caused damage to our school and your rainstorms have stopped our students from attending classes."

"Now that I have my treasures, I will be on my way," Karen said. "And don't try to stop me. I am the one who is controlling these storms. I have all the power. If you let me go, you will have peace on the campus. This is your choice. I control it all."

Before they could respond, the skies darkened and lightning struck the clock tower attached to the Main Hall. Karen looked up in shock.

"Guess you can't control everything." Lucy plunged her sword into a distracted Karen.

A lightning bolt shot through the sky and struck Karen, and she disappeared.

"Where did she go?" Julia asked.

"Was she destroyed?" Brad asked.

Nobody had answers as zombies spawned on the Great Lawn, ripping every door and attacking every student in their path. The campus was overrun with zombies. Julia held her breath to avoid the strong smell of rotting flesh. She grabbed the last bit of potions from her inventory, splashing them on the zombies that circled around her. She let out a large breath as she battled three zombies with her sword. Emma raced to her side and helped Julia escape.

"Mia said she saw Karen," Emma called out to Julia.

"Where?" Julia asked, but she couldn't hear Emma's reply because she was destroying a zombie that stood inches away from her. "What did you say?" Julia asked.

"Karen is in—" Emma said as a skeleton's arrow pierced her unarmored arm and she was destroyed.

Julia turned around to see the skeleton standing behind her, and before she had a chance to defend herself, she also fell victim to the skeleton's arrow. Julia spawned in her bed. She could see Emma sitting up in her bed.

"The skeleton got you too?" Emma asked.

"Yes," Julia replied, "but you have to tell me where Karen is hiding."

"I saw her in the dining hall," Emma said. "I think Mia and Cayla have trapped her over there."

"We have to go there," Julia said.

The duo sprinted under soggy skies, slipping on the grass as they sprinted toward the dining hall. Cayla called out to them, "We've got her here. Come here!"

Karen was standing by a counter in the cafeteria as Mia, Cayla's mom, and Brad surrounded her. Cayla's mom was interrogating Karen. "Tell us how you are controlling these storms. We all know that curses don't really exist in the Overworld."

"They don't?" Karen smiled.

"No," Cayla's mom replied. "We need to know how you've done this. If you don't tell us—"

"What are you going to do to me?" Karen snickered. "Put me in prison?"

Lucy stormed into the dining hall. "Yes, we would. Don't laugh. We've done it to other criminals."

"I'm not a criminal," Karen defended herself. "I'm a treasure hunter."

A zombie ripped the door to the dining hall from the hinges and lumbered into the center of the dining hall.

Julia gasped as an army of zombies marched into the dining hall with their arms extended and mouths gaping in search of new flesh.

Chapter 16
ACCIDENTAL ANSWERS

The zombies gathered the dropped weapons from their conquests and were carrying diamond swords, diamond armor, bows and arrows, and clutching unknown potions.

Karen laughed. "Looks like you have some unwanted company."

Julia fearlessly sprinted toward the zombies as she struck each with her sword, but she was no match for an army of armed zombies and was destroyed. When she awoke in her bed, she was shocked to see the sun was shining. She rushed toward the window and saw students standing on the Great Lawn.

Cayla rushed into Julia's room. "She's missing."

"Who's missing?" Julia asked.

"Karen. She escaped in the middle of the zombie battle," Cayla explained.

Cayla's mom appeared at the door. "We have to find Karen. I know she is controlling these storms, and we have to stop her."

"Do you think she's back on Mushroom Island?" Julia asked.

Lucy, Henry, and Max walked into Julia's room. Lucy announced, "I want you guys to find Karen. I think Henry and Max should join you. I will stay here with Steve and watch the campus."

"I can't believe she got away," Brad said as he walked into the dorm room.

The small room was crowded with people, and Julia felt overwhelmed. She was upset that she was destroyed by the zombie and wasn't there to stop Karen from escaping. Yet Julia knew she couldn't focus on what happened; she had to plan what to do next. She agreed to go on the journey to find Karen.

Lucy suggested, "I think you should go to Mushroom Island." As Lucy spoke, Johnny sprinted into the room.

"I know where Karen is hiding," Johnny announced breathlessly.

Steve ran into the room. "I was looking all over for you guys. I found something, and I think you should all see it."

"What is it? I think we found Karen," Lucy said.

"This is more important." Steve didn't have time to explain. He simply yelled, "Follow me," and sprinted out of the room.

The gang followed Steve across the campus to a patch of land by the dining hall that was shaded by trees.

"Why are you taking us to the dining hall?" Lucy called out.

"You have to see this!" Steve hollered back, leaning over a hole in the ground. "Look what I found."

Lucy's eyes widened. Julia stood next to her, inhaling deeply, and asked, "Is that a chest? Please don't take anything out of it."

Steve dug around the chest, revealing a redstone wire. "See? I think we've gotten our answer. This is how she's been controlling everything."

"What is that?" Cayla asked.

"It's a redstone wire," Steve said. "And it's attached to a command block." Steve walked the length of the wire until he reached the command block. He slammed his sword against the command block, breaking into pieces. Once it was destroyed, he said, "I have an extremely accurate weather prediction. We're going to have sunny skies from now on."

"I knew there weren't any curses in Minecraft," Cayla's mom said. "I knew she was controlling the storm."

"Well, now that we found out her trick, we have to find her," Lucy said.

"Johnny, where is she?" Henry asked.

There was no reply. Johnny was missing. The gang called out his name as they searched the campus, but he never replied. Julia stopped when she heard a faint cry for help.

"Did anyone hear that?" Julia asked.

"No," Emma said.

"Can we just stand still for a second? I thought I heard someone call out for help," Julia said.

The group huddled together in silence. In the distance they could hear someone call out for help.

"Where is that coming from?" Lucy asked.

"It sounds like Johnny," Emma said.

"Karen must have come back to the campus," Cayla's mom said.

"I'm sure she's really upset that we discovered the redstone wire and the command blocks. Now all of her treasure is vulnerable," Steve said.

"Yes, she has to be on campus," Lucy agreed. "She wouldn't want anybody stealing her valuable treasures."

Steve pointed to the farm. "That's where most of the treasure chests were found. We should head over to the farm."

The gang rushed toward the farm and grabbed shovels from their inventories, digging into the farm's surface.

"Found one," Mia called out.

"Me too," Emma said.

They opened the chests. Mia was the first to yell, "Oh no! It's empty."

"I hope she wasn't able to loot all of the treasure chests," Emma said.

Julia kept digging. She wanted to find a treasure chest that was still filled with treasures. Her shovel banged against a chest. Julia pulled it from the ground and opened it.

"This one is full of diamonds." Julia plucked a diamond from the chest and looked up at the sky. Nothing happened. The sky was sunny. She grabbed another diamond from the chest, but there were no storms.

Lucy smiled. "Steve, you really saved the day by discovering the redstone wire."

"Now, if I could only find Karen," Steve said.

Brad spotted a purple jacket in the distance and called out, "Johnny!"

Johnny screamed, "Help me!"

On further inspection, Julia noticed a diamond sword at Johnny's back, but there was nobody holding it. Julia called to her friends, "Karen is here. She's invisible!"

The gang sprinted toward Johnny and the invisible Karen, but as they sprinted across the campus, Johnny disappeared from their sight.

"Where did he go?" Julia asked.

"I don't know, but we have to find them," Steve said.

Cayla's mom said, "I think they're going back to Mushroom Island. I believe Cayla is hiding treasures in a cave on the island."

"We have to teleport there right now," Lucy said.

"All of us?" Julia said.

"Yes," Lucy replied, as the entire gang readied themselves to teleport to Mushroom Island.

Chapter 17
CONFESSIONS

"Do you see them?" Julia placed a torch on the wall of the dimly lit cave.

"No," Lucy called out, "but I think I see something."

The group walked carefully into the dark, musty cave. "What is it?" Julia asked.

"Come here! It looks like there is a stronghold." Lucy opened a door, revealing a large room made of mossy stone brick. There was a large fountain in the middle of the room.

The gang entered the stronghold. "I bet she's storing her loot in here," Brad remarked.

"It looks like there's a wooden door on the other side of the room," Mia said.

"Should we open it?" Julia asked.

Lucy walked across the room, past the fountain, and opened the wooden door. The minute she opened the door, they could hear someone cry out for help.

"Is that Johnny?" asked Julia, who sprinted through the wooden door and down a hall.

Two red eyes peered at her as Brad called out, "Watch out!"

Julia hit the cave spider, destroying it, but her battle wasn't over yet. Silverfish crawled on the floor of the stronghold, and they bit everyone's feet.

"We have to destroy these silverfish," Mia said as she sipped a potion of strength and passed it along to her friends. "They are slowly depleting our energy."

"Help!" Johnny's cries were louder, but his voice sounded weaker. Julia was worried about him, and crushed the silverfish with her feet as she raced toward the sound of his cries.

"Where are you?" Julia called out to Johnny.

"In the prison."

"Prison?" Julia asked, and she reached a small prison made of iron bars. "How can we get you out of here?" Julia looked at Johnny on the other side of the bars.

The rest of the gang arrived. Brad explained, "We had to battle silverfish."

"We have to get Johnny out of here," Julia looked at him and tried to formulate a plot.

A voice boomed through the stronghold. "How nice. You're trying to save Johnny. Is he your friend now? You guys are so caring."

They turned around to see Karen. Diamond armor covered her green dress, and her red hair flowed over her shoulders. She pointed her diamond sword at the group.

"Give yourself up," Lucy said.

"You've asked me to do that before. Can you give me one reason why I should let you guys put me in a prison?"

"You have no power in the Overworld. We found out how you were controlling the storms on our campus, and we've destroyed your command blocks," Steve said.

Johnny called out, "She has a bunch of other plans. She is trying to take over the Overworld."

"Stop it, Johnny. It's not nice to tell secrets." Karen slammed her sword against the iron bars and Johnny sprinted to a corner of the prison, trying to hide himself from Karen.

"Leave Johnny alone," Steve said, as he told Johnny to teleport to him and get out of the prison cell.

Lucy splashed a potion on Karen, weakening her. "We will find out what your other plans were from Johnny. You're outnumbered. There's no escape."

Tears filled Karen's eyes. "Did you find my treasure chest filled with diamonds on the campus?"

"Why do you want to know?" Lucy asked.

"It was the only one I couldn't remove from the campus. I'd like it," Karen said.

"Are you serious?" Lucy was shocked. "Why in the world do you think we'd give that to you?"

"I'm very attached to my treasures," Karen said.

"You stole them from the students when we attended Minecrafters Academy. You should return them," Cayla's mom said.

"But they're mine. They probably don't even remember that they were stolen," Karen reasoned.

"I think they remember. We should contact all of the students that went to school when we did and let them know they can claim their old treasures," Cayla's mom suggested.

"No, they're mine," Karen screamed.

"You're coming with us," Lucy demanded.

Brad, Emma, Mia, Cayla, Johnny, Henry, and Max all pointed their swords at Karen and surrounded her; she knew there was no escape. Her eyes swelled with tears and her voice cracked as she begged, "I know what I did was wrong. Okay. I confess. Can you let me go?"

"No," Lucy said. "You're going to the bedrock prison on our campus. I will make sure you have a prison cell with a window, so you can watch as all the people you stole from come and claim their old treasures."

"But they're mine. All mine," Karen cried, as they forced her to teleport to Minecrafters Academy.

Chapter 18
FARM LIFE

When the last treasure chest was accounted for and the campus was at peace with Karen inside the bedrock prison, Steve started to work on the campus farm. His students, Nick and Jaime, joined the crew as they dug holes and created a new irrigation system.

Steve placed the irrigation system underneath the dirt, explaining each step to creating a working farm. "Another important aspect to farming is seeds," Steve said as he placed seeds down for an apple tree.

"I can't wait to eat the apples from the tree," Emma said.

"It takes a while," Steve said. "It's best if we don't focus on the seeds we planted, but what we else we can do to improve the farm. Sure, we have to tend to the seeds, but if we watch or wait for them, it won't be the best use of our time."

Everyone agreed. Nick said, "Yeah, watching grass grow is boring."

"Yes," Steve said and then asked, "What else would you like to plant on the campus?"

"Potatoes," Emma said.

"Carrots," Mia added.

Julia asked, "Once we've completed the farm and have our first harvest, can we celebrate with a dinner on campus where we serve all of the fresh vegetables from our garden?"

"What a fantastic idea," Steve said.

The sun shone as the gang worked on the farm. Lucy walked over to the group and commended them on their good work. "I hear there's a competition in the Overworld for the best farm. Should I enter this one?"

"Please, I don't want to be in another competition," Emma confessed. She had had her share of competitions with the Minecrafters Academic Olympics.

Steve said, "We just started working on the farm, and we'd like to enjoy it first before we share it with the world."

"That makes sense," Lucy said. "But keep up the good work. I'm glad you were able to join us for this school year, Steve."

"Me too," Steve said.

Cayla said, "I know we're far from Mushroom Island, but is it possible for us to grow mushrooms on our farm?"

"Yes," Steve said. "But due to light's impact on their growth, we have to plant them in a structure."

Cayla looked up at the sky. "Since we have a long time before it's night, can we start the mushroom farm now?"

"Certainly," Steve said, and asked the others if they would be interested in constructing the mushroom farm.

"If it involves building and farming, I'm totally in," Julia said. Brad agreed.

Everyone was excited to learn how to grow mushrooms.

"We need torches. We can't have monsters spawn on our mushroom farm. As I said, there is a delicate balance of lighting to get the mushrooms growing properly," Steve said.

The gang pulled torches from their inventories and worked together to build the structure for the mushrooms to grow properly. The sun was out, and Julia smiled as she built the two-block-tall structure. Julia couldn't wait for their crops to grow and to share their food with the other students. With all the drama behind them, the gang was excited for the rest of the school year at Minecrafters Academy.

READ ON FOR AN EXCITING SNEAK PEEK AT THE NEXT BOOK IN

Winter Morgan's Unofficial Minecrafters Academy series

Chapter 1
GEARING UP FOR GRADUATION

Julia walked toward the familiar dorm room that she had called home during the past few years at Minecrafters Academy. Recently, every time Julia entered the dorms, she felt sad. Graduation was a short while away, and Julia was dreading it. She loved being at Minecrafters Academy and would miss it. Although she knew that her real life was in the cold biome, she was enjoying being a student and spending time with her roommates, Mia and Emma.

Julia entered the room and called out, "Mia, are you ready?"

Mia stood by the closet, filling up a chest with extra supplies from her inventory. "Yes, I'm so excited. I can't believe the farm is completed." Mia closed the chest.

"You worked really hard on the farm." Julia smiled.

"It was all Steve," Mia explained. "He's such a great teacher. Now that I have these new skills, I've contacted a few people who've asked me to build farms for them."

"But when will you find the time?" Julia asked. "We have our schoolwork."

"Julia, you know we only have a short time until this is all over. I start working when school is finished," Mia said. "I'm excited to get back to the real world and start working on farms."

Julia couldn't understand why Mia was so excited to graduate and start a life as a farmer. If Julia had been given the option of extending her time at school, she'd stay at Minecrafters Academy for a few more years. Unlike Mia, Julia was in was no great rush to go out into the Overworld. Yet Julia was happy for her friend Mia. "Wow, that's impressive. I can't believe you already have clients lined up after you leave school."

"They're just small jobs," Mia replied modestly, "but it's a start."

"I have no idea what I'm going to do after graduation," Julia confessed. "In fact, I'm not looking forward to it at all. I'll miss living with you and Emma, and having Cayla down the hall."

Emma walked in and, having overheard them, admitted, "I feel the same way. I'm going to miss you guys. It's been so much fun living with you, and we make a great team."

Cayla sprinted into the room with Brad. "Guys," she said. "We're going to be really late."

"We don't want to disappoint Steve," Brad told them. "I think he wants us to stand next to him as he cuts the ribbon."

Mia looked out the window. "There's already a large crowd standing next to the farm. I think we should hurry."

The group rushed toward the farm and arrived as the opening ceremony was about to begin. Steve called out to the crowd, "I'd like the volunteers to join me as I cut the ribbon."

Mia looked over at Emma. "We made it just in time."

The gang weaved through the crowd, making their way toward Steve. Julia looked at the large red mushrooms that grew from the structure she'd constructed with Brad, and was glad that Mia suggested she volunteer at the farm.

"I'm proud to announce that the school farm is completed. However, this doesn't mean that we will stop working on it. It does mean that we've yielded crops from our first harvest and we will feast on these treats tonight on the great lawn. Everyone is invited to join us as we share our abundant crops!" Steve said.

The crowd cheered, but hushed when Steve spoke again. "I have another announcement. I'm sad to say that this is my last year at Minecrafters Academy. I've enjoyed being a visiting teacher, but I must get back to my wheat farm."

Lucy stood next to Steve. "It was great to have you be a part of the Minecrafters Academy community. I hope you come back to join us soon."

Hearing those words, Steve smiled and cut the red ribbon, inviting everyone to view the garden.

Steve asked the volunteers, “Will you stay and help me pick crops from the garden for the feast?”

The gang agreed. After the crowds cleared, they picked potatoes, carrots, apples, and other crops. Emma stood by the mushrooms. “I’m so glad we can finally have mushrooms. I’ve been craving them ever since we got back from Mushroom Island.”

“After school ends, you can come visit me at Mushroom Island,” Cayla suggested.

Julia asked, “Can I come too?”

“Yes, everyone is invited,” Cayla said. “You’ve been to my house and you know it has more than enough room for all of my friends.”

Julia was happy that her friends at school wanted to keep in contact with her, but she knew once they got back to their old lives, it would be hard to keep in touch.

When the table overflowed with fruit and other crops, Steve signaled that they were done. “I think we have enough. This is going to be an epic feast.”

Steve was right. The feast was epic and rather gluttonous. Steve and the staff cooked chicken, beef, cookies, and cakes. Emma walked over to Julia, whose plate was piled high with food. “This is amazing.”

Julia swallowed her chicken. “Yes, what a great way to celebrate all of the work we’ve done for the garden.”

Mia and Steve joined them. Steve smiled. “I still can’t get over this amazing feast.”

Mia called Lucy over and asked, "Can we make this an annual tradition?"

"That's a great idea," Lucy replied.

"Perfect," Mia said. "It's nice to know that people will celebrate the farm when we're no longer students here."

Nick and Jamie walked over to them. Nick asked, "We did a good job, right?"

"The feast is great, but it's not just our work. A lot of people were involved. Also, they're going to make this an annual tradition," Mia said.

"Wow," Jamie exclaimed. "That's so cool."

Julia tried to imagine all the new students dining at the feast, but it was too hard. She looked up at the sky. The sun was starting to set, and she knew the feast would be over soon.

As everyone mingled, Lucy called out, "Before you finish your meal, I have an announcement."

The partygoers walked over to Lucy as she spoke. "As you all know, graduation is approaching. I will be choosing a class speaker who will have the honor of giving a speech at this event. This is a position that means a lot to the school so we will do an extensive search for the speaker who best represents the school's values."

A student asked, "How will you conduct the search?"

Lucy replied, "Good question. There are many activities that will take place where we will evaluate students."

Julia's stomach started to hurt when she heard Lucy utter the word *competition*, and she wished she hadn't eaten so much chicken. Julia disliked competition. After all the drama with the Minecrafters Academic Olympics, Julia wasn't in the mood for another contest.

"What type of evaluations?" Julia questioned.

"I don't want to go into specifics now, but I will hold an assembly tomorrow morning after breakfast where I will go over everything. That said, in addition to the evaluations, I will also review your overall achievements at Minecrafters Academy and how you work well with others. As you know, working well with others is a huge part of success at this school. If you demonstrate that ability, you will be on the top of my list. I will continue this talk tomorrow," Lucy said, and wished everyone a good night.

Students didn't pay attention to the setting sun. They were fixating on the upcoming competition. Lucy's announcement at the end of the meal kept everyone at the feast longer than they should have stayed. Everyone was busy chatting about which student might be chosen for the role of class speaker, and everyone lost track of the time until Nick called out, "Watch out!"

A skeleton army marched across the campus, toting bows and arrows.

Chapter 2
PICK ME

Two block-headed skeletons stood inches from Julia. Arrows flew toward her and before she could put on her armor or grab a sword, an arrow sliced through her arm. Julia wailed as she reached into her inventory for her sword, barely grasping the weapon. Another arrow pierced her other arm. Julia fumbled with her sword and it dropped to the ground.

A zombie spawned and lumbered toward the dropped sword. Julia tried to stop the newly spawned beast, knowing that an armed zombie alongside a skeleton attack would be almost impossible to defeat. She made it over to her dropped weapon. With a renewed energy, she slammed her sword against the zombie's rotten flesh, holding her breath to avoid the odor. With three strikes of her sword, she destroyed the zombie and collected the dropped rotten flesh from the ground. Two arrows flew toward her as she ducked and sprinted toward the skeletons. She plunged her sword into the skeleton's bony body with great force, cracking its rattling frame. She hit both skeletons and was confident she'd defeat them until she felt the sting of arrows pelt her back. Julia awoke in her room, calling out for her roommates, but the room was silent.

Julia placed a torch on her wall, raced to the window, and looked out at the campus. It was dark, but she could see three greenish and rather ghoulish creepers sneaking up behind Mia and Emma. She tried to shout for them to turn around, but it was too late. Julia watched as the fiery creatures exploded and destroyed her friends.

"Julia," Emma called out as she spawned in her bed.

"What happened?" asked a confused Mia.

"You were destroyed by creepers," Julia informed her.

Mia sat up. "Should we stay here for the night?"

Emma asked in a sleepy haze, "Maybe we should go out and help everyone?"

A loud voice was heard throughout the campus. "Head back to your rooms until morning. I repeat, everyone stay in your rooms."

"Was that Lucy?" Mia asked.

"I think so," Emma said.

Julia crawled back in the bed, covering herself with a blue blanket, and wished her friends a good night. Of course, getting to sleep wasn't easy. Julia was distracted by the battle outside her window. The roommates were also awakened by alerts telling them hostile mobs were close by, which they decided to ignore due to Lucy's instructions. Even though Lucy had asked the students to head back to the dorms, Julia knew some people were fighting the hostile mobs that crowded on the great lawn. Julia tried to fall asleep. She even counted sheep, but it didn't work. She was wide-awake.

"Do you think this was one of Lucy's tests?" Mia asked.

Julia was glad she wasn't the only one having trouble sleeping. "What do you mean?"

"When Lucy made that important announcement right before dusk, she knew she was putting us in jeopardy. Maybe she wanted to see how we'd handle the battle," Mia said.

"That makes sense," said Emma, who admitted that she couldn't sleep due to the excitement from the battle.

Even if they could have slept, it wouldn't have been for long because, almost instantly, zombies ripped their door from its hinges and down the hall, Cayla screamed for help.

"Zombies!" Emma jumped up from her bed, quickly putting on her armor. The other girls followed Emma, clutching their swords as they rushed toward the door.

A vacant-eyed zombie reeking of fetid-smelling, rotting flesh raised its arms and readied itself for an attack against Julia's roommates. She swung her sword, hitting the zombie, and its flesh oozed out its body. With a second strike she destroyed the zombie, and decided not to pick up the rotten flesh that dropped on the floor. Instead she sprinted toward Cayla's room as her friends battled the remaining zombies. Cayla's cries grew louder as Julia raced down the hall to help her.

The zombies had ripped Cayla's door off the hinges and were surrounding Cayla. An exhausted Cayla struck out at the group of four zombies with her sword, but she was outnumbered and destroyed, only to spawn and fight the same battle all over again. Julia surprised the zombies and struck one with her sword. Cayla had weakened the zombies, making them easier to battle. One by one, Julia slammed her sword into their backs, obliterating them.

"Thanks," Cayla said. "It was so awful. Every time I was destroyed, I'd have to fight the zombies again. I couldn't do it alone."

"Watch out!" Julia cried as two creepers spawned in the open closet behind Cayla. Julia quickly traded in her sword for a bow and arrow and aimed at the creepers, striking each one. They exploded inches from Cayla.

"Wow, you saved me again," Cayla thanked Julia.

"We have to craft a new door quickly." Julia grabbed wood from her inventory and started to build a new door to replace the one that the zombies had destroyed.

Cayla helped Julia construct the door. When it was finished she said, "We make a great team."

"You certainly do," a voice called out from the hall.

Cayla and Julia turned around to find Lucy standing in the hall. Julia was surprised.

"It's time to go to bed," Lucy informed them. "Julia, please head back to your room."

As Julia walked back to her dorm room, she wondered if Mia was correct in thinking this night battle might be a part of the competition for class speaker. If this was a test, did she win?